The Petal Fairies

For Lily Bisseker,
with lots of love

Special thanks to
Sue Mongredien

ORCHARD BOOKS
338 Euston Road, London NW1 3BH
Orchard Books Australia
Level 17/207 Kent Street, Sydney, NSW 2000
A Paperback Original

First published in 2007 by Orchard Books
Rainbow Magic is a registered trademark of Working Partners Limited.
Series created by Working Partners Limited, London W6 0QT

A CIP catalogue record for this book is available
from the British Library.

ISBN 978 1 84616 459 0
1 3 5 7 9 10 8 6 4 2

Printed in China

Orchard Books is a division of Hachette Children's Books

www.orchardbooks.co.uk

Louise
the Lily
Fairy

by Daisy Meadows

ORCHARD BOOKS

www.rainbowmagic.co.uk

The Fairyland Palace

Blossom Hall

Fairy Garden

Leafley Village

Visitors' Centre

Jack Frost's Ice Castle

Blossom Lake

Picnic Spot

The Park

Petal Perfection Flower Shop

Blossom Village High St

Rainbow Falls Gardens

Chaney Court Flower Show

I need the magic petals' powers,
To give my castle garden flowers.
And so I use my magic well
To work against the fairies' spell.

From my wand ice magic flies,
Frosty bolt through fairy skies.
And this crafty spell I weave
To bring the petals back to me.

Contents

Woodland Walk

"Blossom Lake this way!" Rachel Walker
called out, seeing the wooden sign
ahead. Buttons, her dog, trotted by her
side, sniffing at the trees and brambles.

Kirsty Tate smiled happily as she,
Rachel, their parents and Buttons
turned left off the trail, and started
heading deep into the trees.

She was so glad they were all spending the Easter holidays together this year. It made her think about the first time she had met Rachel, when the two families had stayed next door to each other one summer, on Rainspell Island. Since then, Kirsty and Rachel had become best friends – and they always had the most exciting adventures whenever they were together!

The two families were staying at
an old manor house, Blossom Hall,
for a whole week, and today they'd
come out to visit Blossom Lake.

"I can't wait to see the lake,"
Kirsty said, as she, Rachel and
Buttons led the way down a sloping
path through the trees. "There was
a picture in Mum's guidebook, and
it looked really pretty."

Rachel grinned at Kirsty. "I wonder what else we'll see today," she said in a low voice.

Kirsty knew exactly what her friend meant. "Oh, I really hope we meet another Petal Fairy," she whispered in reply. "But remember what the Fairy Queen always says – that we have to wait for the magic to come to us."

Kirsty and Rachel shared a wonderful secret. They were friends with the fairies! They had had all sorts of fairy adventures together, and just two days ago, they'd found themselves starting a whole new adventure, this time helping the seven Petal Fairies.

"Ah, there's the lake," said Kirsty's mum, making the girls jump. Both Kirsty and Rachel had been so busy thinking about fairies that they hadn't realised they were coming out of the forest. There, ahead of them, lay a stretch of blue water, with sunlight sparkling on its surface.

They came out into the sunshine near the water's edge. "It's lovely," Rachel sighed happily, gazing at the woods that surrounded the water. "Is that an island in the middle?"

"Certainly looks like one," her dad said, shielding his eyes from the sun as he looked over to where Rachel was pointing. "Now don't go scaring the ducks, Buttons!" he said, quickly catching Buttons. The excited dog was rushing towards the ducks who were dabbling in the weeds

at the side of the lake. "I think I'd better put you on a lead," he added, clipping it onto Buttons's collar.

"Ooh, look!" Kirsty said excitedly. Her eye had been caught by a small jetty at the edge of the lake, a little further along the path from where they were standing. There was a small wooden boathouse next to it, and a few rowing boats tied up alongside. Kirsty turned to Rachel, her eyes shining. "Fancy taking a boat out?"

"Can we, Mum?" Rachel asked, gazing pleadingly at her parents.

The four adults looked at one
another. "I don't see why not,"
Mrs Walker replied. "As long as you
can borrow life jackets. You two can
hire a boat while we take a stroll
around the lake."

"Great!" Kirsty cheered. "Come
on, Rachel!"

Mrs Tate took the girls over to the

boathouse, where
a friendly man
untied a boat
for them and
showed them
how to put on
their life jackets.
"Be careful,
won't you girls?"
Mrs Tate said.

"Don't worry," Rachel replied, sitting carefully on the wooden seat and feeling a thrill go through her as the boat bobbed gently on the water. "We'll be fine."

"Thanks, Mum. See you later!" Kirsty called.

"Happy sailing," replied Mrs Tate. She gave them a last wave and went off with the other adults.

"Who's going to row, then?" the
boatman asked.

"We'll take it in turns," Rachel said.
"Do you want to go first, Kirsty?"

Kirsty nodded happily and the
boatman passed her a pair of oars, and
helped slide them into the rowlocks.

"Thanks," Kirsty said, staring excitedly across the lake. There were lots of plants floating in clumps on the surface of the water, and she used an oar to pull one closer to her. The leaves of the plant were round and shiny. "Are these lily pads?" she asked the boatman curiously.

He nodded. "That's how Blossom Lake got its name," he said. "Because so many lilies blossom here. They're usually out by now, as this is such a sheltered spot, but they're late this year." His weatherbeaten face creased into a smile. "You'll have to come back and see them when they're in full bloom," he told the girls. "It's quite a sight!"

The boatman pushed the rowing boat out into the lake, and the girls gave

 each other a knowing glance. "We know why the lilies are late to blossom," Rachel said quietly, once they were out of earshot.

"It's because Louise the Lily Fairy's magic petal is still missing!"

Kirsty nodded as she pulled on the oars. On the first day of their holiday, the girls had met Tia the Tulip Fairy, who had told them that the Petal Fairies' seven magic petals were all lost in the human world. Naughty Jack Frost had sent his sneaky goblin servants to steal the petals, so that he could use their special magic to make flowers grow around his freezing ice castle. But when the

Petal Fairies had used some of their magic to rescue the petals, it had mixed with Jack Frost's spell to cause a huge explosion – sending the petals flying out of Fairyland! Without their magic petals, the Petal Fairies were unable to help the flowers bloom and grow, so it wasn't just the lilies that were late to bloom this year. None of the flowers were growing properly. The girls had vowed to help the fairies find their petals and return them to Fairyland. They had already found Tia's Tulip Petal and Pippa's Poppy Petal, which meant that some

flowers were starting to bloom
brightly again, but five magic
petals were still lost.

Rachel smiled across the boat at
Kirsty. "Are you thinking what
I'm thinking?" she asked.

Kirsty grinned. "I'm thinking that
I hope we find the Lily Petal today!"
she replied.

Blossom Lake really is gorgeous,
Rachel thought as Kirsty rowed further
into the centre. The water was
shimmering in the sunlight, and
emerald-green dragonflies skimmed
across its surface, while a couple of big
orange fish darted beneath the boat.

"We're getting near the island," Kirsty

said after a little while. "Shall we go
over, and explore it?"

Rachel twisted round in her seat, and
saw the island looming up behind her.
There was a small wooden dock there,
and she could see trees and shrubs
further back. "Good idea," she said.

Kirsty steered them into the dock, and

they tied the boat up carefully and clambered out.

"What a sweet place!" Rachel said, gazing round.

Kirsty agreed. Butterflies fluttered between the trees, and birds were singing. "Come on, let's explore!" she said.

The two girls set off on a rough track that led away from the water, through the trees. They hadn't got very far when they heard a noise.
Pssst!

"What was that?" Kirsty whispered, stopping and looking round.

Rachel grinned. "Over there," she said, pointing at a nearby shrub, and then waving at it.

Kirsty stared in surprise. Why was Rachel waving at a bush? Then she chuckled as she spotted the tiny fairy who was peeping out from between the leaves. Kirsty and Rachel had met all the Petal Fairies on the first day of their holiday, and she recognised who it was at once.

"Hello, Louise!" she said, as she and Rachel hurried over. "We were hoping we'd see you again today."

The fairy beamed and shot up into the air in a burst of pale pink sparkles. "Hello there," she said cheerfully. "I was hoping to see you two as well."

Louise had blonde hair that fell in curls to her shoulders, pinned back with pretty pink hair clips. She wore a pale green dress, with a light pink silk sash, and light green boots that matched her dress.

Her pretty face clouded over for a second as she landed lightly on Rachel's shoulder. "Have you seen the goblins yet? They're on the island, too, and I just heard them saying that they know where my petal is!"

Kirsty's face fell at this news. She never liked running into Jack Frost's goblins, but this time round it was even worse. Jack Frost was so desperate to get his hands on the magic petals that he had given his goblin servants a wand full of his own icy magic to use. Kirsty and Rachel had always been able to outwit the goblins in the past, but it was much harder now that they were armed with a magic wand!

"What does your petal look like?" Rachel asked.

"It's pale pink," Louise told her. "And it helps all the lilies in the world to grow, as well as all the light pink flowers, too."

The girls had learned that each magic petal was responsible for making its own particular type of flower grow, as well as other flowers of the same colour as the petal.

"Where are the goblins?" Kirsty wanted to know.

"They're on the other side of the island," Louise replied. "Follow me!"

She fluttered her gauzy wings and took off into the air. Rachel and Kirsty followed her through the trees. Both girls were feeling rather nervous about the goblins. Kirsty hoped they would be able to find Louise's Lily Petal before one of the goblins spotted it!

After a few minutes, Louise perched on a large bush and motioned for the girls to crouch behind it. Then she put a finger to her lips. "Don't make a sound," she hissed, waving her wand.

A flood of pale pink fairy dust billowed
out from the wand's tip, and
at once, the twigs and
leaves of the bush parted,
making a neat spyhole
for Rachel and Kirsty
to see through.
The girls could
now see that they
were right on the
other side of the
island. The blue
water of the lake
was only a few
steps from their
hiding place, and
Rachel's eyes widened
as she saw a bridge joining
the island to the shore of the lake.

She hadn't noticed that before. Then
she realised that the bridge was made
of ice!

"The goblins have used Jack Frost's

wand to create the
bridge," Louise
confirmed in
a tiny whisper.
"That's how
they got across
to the island in
the first place."
Kirsty couldn't help
marvelling at the icy bridge. It looked
beautiful with the sun shining on it,
making the ice crystals glitter and
twinkle. But as she watched, she
realised that the bridge was dripping.
"It's melting!" she hissed.

Splash! A section of
the bridge
collapsed into
the lake.

Louise
nodded. "It
certainly is," she
said. "They'll have to
magic up another bridge if they want
to get off the island again."

Rachel was frowning. "What are the
goblins doing?" she asked in a low voice.

The girls and Louise stared at the
strange sight. One of the goblins was
up in a tree that stood on the edge
of the island, with its branches
overhanging the water. The goblin was
dangling upside down from a branch
by his huge green feet. Underneath

him, in a sort of goblin chain, swung six other goblins, one after another, each holding onto the feet of the goblin below. The goblin at the bottom of the chain, who had particularly large ears, was straining forward. He  seemed to be trying to reach something on the surface of the lake but his hands were blocking the girls' view.

Just then, he twisted himself round to call up instructions to the others, and Kirsty and Rachel gasped as they saw exactly what he'd been trying to get.

Louise's pale pink Lily Petal was right there on a lily pad, just centimetres from the big-eared goblin. And as the girls watched, the wind sent the lily pad sailing even closer to him. The friends held their breath. Any moment now, the goblin was going to turn back and see that the Lily Petal was right under his nose!

Splash and Grab

"Don't touch that petal!" Rachel
yelled, charging out from the girls'
hiding place with Kirsty and Louise
close behind her.

The goblins were startled by the
appearance of the girls. The one
holding the big-eared goblin's feet let
go of him in surprise, and there was

a great splash as he fell into the lake.

Kirsty, Rachel and Louise couldn't help laughing as he staggered out of the water, dripping wet. He shook himself like a dog, sending water and clumps of weed flying everywhere, much to the amusement of his friends who were still hanging from the tree.

The wet goblin didn't seem to mind his friends' laughter though. He was too busy waving the pink petal in the air, with a look of triumph. "Look what I've got!" he cried boastfully. "And I'm going to deliver it to Jack Frost personally. Oho, he's going to be very pleased with me!"

Louise stamped her foot in dismay, sending a little puff of pale pink sparkles floating up into the air. "Oh, no," she wailed. "I can't believe he's got my Lily Petal!"

The other goblins scrambled down from the tree. "Let's have a look at it, then!" called a squinty-eyed goblin who was holding Jack Frost's magic wand.

But the big-eared goblin clutched
the petal proudly to his chest. "No
chance," he retorted. "I'm looking
after this myself!"

"That petal belongs to Louise the Lily
Fairy," Kirsty said, in her fiercest voice.
"Now give it back!"

"No way!" the big-eared goblin
sneered, and he dodged out of the way
as Rachel tried to grab him.

"Run for it!" ordered the goblin with the wand, and at his words, all seven of the goblins hurtled past the girls at top speed.

Kirsty, Rachel and Louise chased after them, through the trees and back to the other side of the island. It wasn't long before the goblins reached the dock, and Rachel and Kirsty heard cries of glee as they spotted the girls' rowing boat.

"Just what we needed!" one cheered.

"And the bridge is melting, so those
rotten girls will be trapped!" guffawed
a second one.

Rachel stared in horror as she
approached the dock and saw the
goblins clustered round the little boat.

"Hey, that's ours!"
she yelled, but
the goblins were
already hopping
aboard, waving
cheekily to
the girls.
"Too late!"
grinned the
big-eared goblin,
as one of his friends untied the rope and
pushed the boat away from the side.

"Bye bye!" chortled the goblin with the wand, clutching his sides as if it was the funniest thing ever.

Kirsty and Rachel could only stand and watch them go from the edge of the dock. "Oh, no," groaned Kirsty. "Without our boat, we're stuck here. What are we going to do?"

A Wave of Panic

"I'm going to turn you into fairies, of course!" Louise declared brightly. She waved her wand over the girls, and a fountain of lily-scented fairy dust swirled all around them. Instantly, Kirsty and Rachel felt themselves shrinking down to fairy size.

Rachel fluttered her delicate wings

and glared at the goblins. "What are we waiting for?" she cried. "Follow that boat!"

The three fairies flitted across the water towards the rowing boat. Kirsty could see that the goblins weren't going very fast, and as she drew nearer to the boat, she realised why: the goblins could never do anything without arguing.

"I should be captain!" the goblin with the petal yelled crossly. "I've got the magic petal."

"No, I should be," the squinty-eyed goblin argued. "I've got the wand!"

The goblin with the petal jumped to his feet, glaring, and the boat started rocking dangerously in the water.

"Hey!"

"Sit down!"

"Stop it!" his friends shouted in alarm, pulling him back down.

"Call yourself a captain? You nearly had us in the water, then, you idiot!" one of them jeered.

"So I'd better be captain, then," the squinty-eyed goblin insisted.

"Then I'll have the oars," announced a skinny goblin.

"No, I want them!" protested the tall goblin next to him.

"You can have one oar each!" snapped the squinty-eyed goblin, bossily. "That's captain's orders, and you're not allowed to argue!"

The fairies hovered behind the boat as the two goblins began rowing. Unfortunately, they were both moving their oars in different directions, and the little boat went round and round in circles.

The squinty-eyed goblin sighed. "Useless! Useless!" he complained. "You have to row at the same time, and in the same way! Idiots!"

At long last, the rowers seemed to get the hang of it and the boat slowly moved away across the lake.

"I wonder where they're heading," Rachel said thoughtfully. "Surely it would be too risky for them to go back to the jetty near the boathouse? What if the boatman spotted them?"

Kirsty narrowed her eyes as she noticed the boat veering off in a different direction. "Look," she said, pointing to a spot on the shore of the lake that was a little further along from the boathouse. "There's a beach there. I bet that's where they're going. Let's fly ahead and wait for them to arrive."

The other two
nodded, and they
all flew to the
small stretch of
beach. They landed
on the sand, and as
the boat drew near,
Louise waved her wand and turned
Rachel and Kirsty back into girls.

"What took you so long?" Rachel
asked the goblins cheekily, as the boat
approached the shore.

The big-eared
goblin groaned
when he saw her
standing there.
"Oh, not you
again!" he said,
pulling a face.

The goblin with the wand grinned.
"Don't worry, I can take care of them,"
he boasted. He pointed the wand at
the girls and shouted, "Magic, make
a great big wave, to wash those pesky
girls...away-ve!"

"'Away-ve'?" Kirsty snorted. "That's
a terrible rhyme!"

"They're not getting any better at
making up spells," Rachel agreed.

"But that doesn't stop them from
working!" Louise cried
in alarm. For there,
rolling out of the
sea towards them,
like a huge wall
of water, was the
most enormous wave
they had ever seen.

Rachel and Kirsty started to back away hurriedly, but they couldn't move fast enough.

"It's coming in too quickly," Rachel panted. "Help!"

Lost and Found

Louise reacted in a split-second, throwing fairy dust over the girls. In the twinkling of an eye, they were transformed into fairies again and were able to zoom high into the air, safely out of reach of the wave.

"Phew," Rachel sighed. "Thanks, Louise. That wave is enormous!"

"And it's just about to hit the
goblins," Kirsty said. "Look!"

The three fairies all stared down to
see that the goblins were on the verge
of getting caught up in their own spell.
They were all still in their boat,
shouting and pointing as the magic
wave drew nearer.

The wave rushed at them, picking
up the boat and tipping it right over.

It swept the boat up onto the beach and then left it there, upside down, as the waters receded into the lake.

"Hey!"

"It's all dark!"

"Who turned the lights out?" cried the goblins who were trapped underneath.

A great banging and thumping started up, and the three friends looked at one another, wondering what to do next.

"Those goblins should give that wand back to Jack Frost," Kirsty said.

"They've got themselves into big trouble with it this time!" Rachel agreed.

Louise nodded. "It's lucky that I'm kind-hearted enough to take pity on them!" she said, swooping down towards the boat with Rachel and Kirsty flying after her.

Louise muttered a few magic words and twirled her wand over the boat. Pale pink glittery magic streamed from her wand, and then the rowing boat slowly tipped onto one side and fell the right way up on the sand.

The goblins got to their feet, coughing and spluttering, and shaking water off themselves.

"I'm soaked," one muttered crossly,
pulling a face. "Stupid boat, stupid
wave. And where's that petal anyway?"

The goblin who'd been holding onto
the petal looked dismayed. "It got
washed out of my hands by that
wave," he moaned, searching around
for the petal. Then, not seeing it
anywhere, he turned on the goblin with
the wand. "It's all your fault!" he
snapped. "You and your stupid spell!"

"My stupid spell?" the
goblin with the wand
replied. "Your stupid
fingers, you mean.
Should have hung
onto the petal a bit
tighter, shouldn't you?
I knew we shouldn't

have trusted you to look after it!"

As the goblins argued on and on about whose fault losing the petal was, something caught Rachel's eye. She fluttered over the water for a closer look, then beckoned her friends over, beaming.

"I've found the petal!" she whispered. "Look! There it is, floating on the lake!"

Lovely Lilies

Rachel swooped down to pick up the petal, but it was wet and heavy, so her friends flew to help.

A groan of dismay went up from the goblins on the beach when they saw what was happening. "Those wretched fairies are going to get the petal now!" the big-eared goblin

complained, stamping his foot in rage.
The goblin with the wand lifted it

grandly into the air.
"Don't worry," he
announced. "I'll take
care of—" But the
other goblins jumped
on him before he could
say another word.

"NOOOO!" they
all cried together,
as the girls laughed.
"No more spells!
Look what
happened the last
time!" the skinny
goblin complained,
still shaking water
from his ears.

Louise waved her wand over the Lily
Petal, shrinking it down to its Fairyland
size with a happy smile on her face.
Then, holding onto it tightly, she flew
back to the goblins. "Next time, don't
take things that don't belong to you!"
she scolded. "And you can tell Jack
Frost that, too!"

The goblins ignored her,
and stomped off with
grumpy faces.

Louise hugged
the girls
gratefully.
"Thanks so
much, girls," she
said. "Now I'd better
take my petal straight
back to Fairyland, where it belongs."

She pointed her wand at the girls
and a cloud of fairy dust whirled
up from nowhere.

All of a sudden, Rachel and Kirsty
found themselves their normal size again,
and sitting in the rowing boat, with the
oars in place!

Louise smiled. "I'll just get you back
onto the lake," she said, with another
wave of her wand.

Rachel and Kirsty grinned in delight
as the boat slid gently down the beach,
all on its own, and back into the water.

"Thanks, Louise!" Kirsty called.

Rachel waved to the
little fairy and
then took hold
of the oars.
"Bye!" she
called,
blinking
as Louise
vanished in
a pale pink puff
of sparkles.

Rachel rowed the
boat back across the lake towards the
boathouse. Luckily, Louise's fairy magic
had completely dried the little boat, so

the boatman would have no idea that one of his rowing boats had been tossed upside down in a giant wave.

"Perfect timing," Kirsty said happily as they approached the boathouse. "Look – there are our parents."

Rachel turned to see the four adults strolling towards the boathouse, at the end of their walk. "I bet we've had a more exciting time than they have," she grinned. "I bet... Oh!"

She broke off in surprise as she saw a single pink water lily unfold on a lily pad nearby. "The lilies are blooming!" she cheered. "There's a white one," Kirsty said, pointing. "Oh, and another pink one. They're all opening!" The two friends smiled at one another. "Louise's Petal Magic is working again," Rachel exclaimed. "That was quick!"

It was glorious rowing back through all the beautiful pink and white lilies. When they reached the boathouse, the boatman was shaking his head in amazement.

"And there was me saying you'd have to come back to see them in full bloom," he chuckled. "It's almost magical the way they've all started opening up now!"

The girls nodded, but Kirsty didn't dare look at Rachel in case she burst out laughing with delight. *Almost magical? It* was *magical!* she thought with a smile.

"Hello!" called Mr and Mrs Walker, striding up with Buttons alongside.

"Had a good time?" asked Kirsty's dad.

Rachel looked at Kirsty. "Oh, yes," she said, grinning. "We've had a fairy good time!"

The Petal Fairies

Louise the Lily Fairy has got
her magic petal back. Now Rachel
and Kirsty must help

Charlotte the Sunflower Fairy

Win Rainbow Magic goodies!

In every book in the Rainbow Magic Petal Fairies series (books 43-49) there is a hidden picture of a petal with a secret letter in it. Find all seven letters and re-arrange them to make a special Petal Fairies word, then send it to us. Each month we will put the entries into a draw and select one winner to receive a Rainbow Magic Sparkly T-shirt and Goody Bag!

Send your entry on a postcard to Rainbow Magic Fun Day Competition, Orchard Books, 338 Euston Road, London NW1 3BH. Australian readers should write to Hachette Children's Books, Level 17/207 Kent Street, Sydney, NSW 2000. New Zealand readers should write to Rainbow Magic Competition, 4 Whetu Place, Mairangi Bay, Auckland, NZ. Don't forget to include your name and address. Only one entry per child. Final draw: 30th April 2008.

Good luck!

Have you checked out the

website at:

www.rainbowmagic.co.uk

by Daisy Meadows

The Rainbow Fairies

The Weather Fairies

The Party Fairies

The Jewel Fairies

The Pet Keeper Fairies

Katie the Kitten Fairy	ISBN	978 1 84616 166 7
Bella the Bunny Fairy	ISBN	978 1 84616 170 4
Georgia the Guinea Pig Fairy	ISBN	978 1 84616 168 1
Lauren the Puppy Fairy	ISBN	978 1 84616 169 8
Harriet the Hamster Fairy	ISBN	978 1 84616 167 4
Molly the Goldfish Fairy	ISBN	978 1 84616 172 8
Penny the Pony Fairy	ISBN	978 1 84616 171 1

The Fun Day Fairies

Megan the Monday Fairy	ISBN	978 184616 188 9
Tallulah the Tuesday Fairy	ISBN	978 1 84616 189 6
Willow the Wednesday Fairy	ISBN	978 1 84616 190 2
Thea the Thursday Fairy	ISBN	978 1 84616 191 9
Freya the Friday Fairy	ISBN	978 1 84616 192 6
Sienna the Saturday Fairy	ISBN	978 1 84616 193 3
Sarah the Sunday Fairy	ISBN	978 1 84616 194 0

Holly the Christmas Fairy	ISBN	978 1 84362 661 9
Summer the Holiday Fairy	ISBN	978 1 84362 960 3
Stella the Star Fairy	ISBN	978 1 84362 869 9
Kylie the Carnival Fairy	ISBN	978 1 84616 175 9
Paige the Pantomime Fairy	ISBN	978 1 84616 047 9
The Rainbow Magic Treasury	ISBN	978 1 84616 209 1

Coming soon:

Flora the Fancy Dress Fairy	ISBN	978 1 84616 505 4

All priced at £3.99. *Holly the Christmas Fairy, Summer the Holiday Fairy, Stella the Star Fairy, Kylie the Carnival Fairy, Paige the Pantomime Fairy* and *Flora the Fancy Dress Fairy* are priced at £5.99. *The Rainbow Magic Treasury* is priced at £12.99.
Rainbow Magic books are available from all good bookshops, or can be ordered direct from the publisher: Orchard Books, PO BOX 29, Douglas IM99 1BQ
Credit card orders please telephone 01624 836000
or fax 01624 837033 or visit our Internet site: www.wattspub.co.uk
or e-mail: bookshop@enterprise.net for details.

To order please quote title, author and ISBN and your full name and address.
Cheques and postal orders should be made payable to 'Bookpost plc.'
Postage and packing is FREE within the UK
(overseas customers should add £2.00 per book).
Prices and availability are subject to change.

Look out for the Dance Fairies!

BETHANY
THE BALLET FAIRY
978-1-84616-490-3

JADE
THE DISCO FAIRY
978-1-84616-491-0

REBECCA
THE ROCK 'N' ROLL FAIRY
978-1-84616-492-7

TASHA
THE TAP DANCE FAIRY
978-1-84616-493-4

JESSICA
THE JAZZ FAIRY
978-1-84616-495-8

SASKIA
THE SALSA FAIRY
978-1-84616-496-5

IMOGEN
THE ICE DANCE FAIRY
978-1-84616-497-2

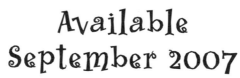

Available September 2007